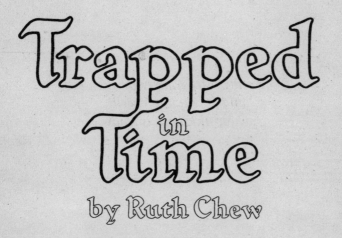

Trapped in Time

by Ruth Chew

Illustrations by the author

SCHOLASTIC INC.
New York Toronto London Auckland Sydney

For my sister Audrey Brixner,
and for Audrey Vagell,
whose nickname is Andy.

Reading level is determined by using
the Spache Readability Formula.
2.2 signifies high second-grade level.

ISBN 0-590-33813-7

12 11 10 9 8 7 6 5 4 3 2 1   2   6 7 8 9/8 0 1/9

Printed in the U.S.A.

1

"HEY, Andy, I'll bet I can beat you to the top of Lookout Mountain." Nathan started up the steep hill in Prospect Park.

"Bet you can't!" Audrey raced after him. Her legs were longer than Nathan's, and she could run faster. But she was carrying their lunch. It was in a plastic shopping bag that bumped against her legs.

Nathan was almost at the top of the hill when he skidded on a patch of dry leaves. He grabbed hold of a big stump to keep from falling.

Crunch! The air was filled with flying dirt. When the cloud of dirt cleared, Audrey saw her brother sitting near the stump. It lay on its side with broken roots sticking out of it. Beside it was a deep hole where the roots had been.

"Are you all right, Nathan?" Audrey came running up the hill.

Nathan stood up and brushed the dirt off his jacket and the seat of his jeans. "My mouth is full of grit, but I guess I'm okay. What happened?"

"You pulled the stump out of the ground." Audrey looked into the hole. "There's something shiny down there."

Nathan went to the edge of the hole. "Maybe it's buried treasure. I'm going to find out." He started climbing down into the hole.

Audrey wanted to know what was down there just as much as he did, but she was older. It would be her fault if anything happened to her little brother. "Come back up here this minute!"

Nathan was hanging onto the broken roots on the side of the hole. He went down until he could reach the shining thing. "It's stuck in the dirt, Andy."

Audrey put down the plastic bag and looked around. In Brooklyn people leave all sorts of things in the park. Audrey pulled a bent umbrella spoke from under a bush. "Can you dig with this?" She leaned over the hole to hand the spoke to her brother.

In a few minutes Nathan dug out the shining thing and rubbed some of the dirt off it. "Andy, it's a watch!"

"You'd better get out of that hole before it caves in," Audrey said.

Nathan put the watch into his pants pocket and began to climb out. Audrey lay on her stomach and reached down to help him. At last he pulled himself over the edge.

Audrey picked up the plastic shopping bag and hung it over her arm. She started running up the hill. Nathan puffed after her.

Audrey got to the top first. She sat down on a bench beside the walk there. "I thought you were going to beat me going up Lookout Mountain."

Nathan grinned. "You win, Andy. Now, let's look at the buried treasure." He sat beside her and took the watch out of his pocket.

Audrey used a clump of weeds to rub the rest of the dirt off the watch. "It's the same color as Mother's ring."

"It's gold!" Nathan said. "That's why it hasn't turned green or black. I learned that from television." He held the watch to his ear. "I wonder if we could get it to tick."

"Try winding it," Audrey said.

"The stem won't turn," Nathan told her. "I don't want to force it."

"Let me have it for a minute." Audrey took the watch. "It has JG written on the back." She turned the watch over and found she could open the glass cover like a little door. "There's a hole in the face of the watch. That must be where you wind it."

Nathan pulled a tiny key out of his pants pocket. "This winds up the toy monkey I bought at the circus."

Audrey held the watch while Nathan tried the key in the hole. It slipped in as if it were made for it. Nathan gave the key three turns. The watch began to tick. He wound it up and put the key back into his pocket. "Now, how do we set the time?"

"Maybe the way Mother sets the cuckoo clock," Audrey said. "What time shall we set it?"

"Twelve o' clock," Nathan told her. "I'm hungry."

Audrey touched the big hand of the watch to push it forward. At once she pulled her finger away. "Nathan, it's setting itself!"

Audrey had to hold onto the watch tightly to keep from dropping it. The big hand was spinning around the dial, with the little hand following. The watch dinged on the hour and the half hour. The hands spun faster and faster. Soon there was no time between dings. The children seemed to have a steady ringing in their ears.

"Andy," Nathan whispered, "the hands are going the wrong way. It's setting itself *backward!*"

2

AUDREY and Nathan watched the spinning hands of the watch until their eyes began to blur. After a while the hands went more slowly. Now they could hear each ding of the watch all by itself. At last both hands were pointing to the *XII*.

The watch dinged twelve times.

Nathan rubbed his eyes. "The park looks different, Andy. I thought we were sitting on a bench."

Audrey stopped staring at the watch and looked around. The park was dark and shadowy, with many more trees than she remembered. Here and there a shaft of September sunlight came through the leaves. The stone walk was just a winding path across the top of Lookout Mountain. And the two children were side by side on a fallen log.

A black and white bird flew from one tree to the next. It sat on a branch to whistle a tune. A breeze rustled the leaves overhead. The only other sound was the ticking of the old watch.

There was no roar of jet planes crossing the sky. Even the noise of traffic going around Park Circle was missing.

"It's so quiet that it's spooky," Nathan said. "Do you know what I think, Andy?"

Audrey nodded. "The watch is magic. And it's done something to the park. I'm not sure what, but I want to find out. Are you scared, Nathan?"

Nathan looked at a patch of red cardinal flowers growing on the hill. A little brown rabbit hopped across the path, bobbing its white tail behind it. "I was scared at first," Nathan said. "But I'm not anymore. Let me have the watch back, Andy."

"I could keep it for you in the pocket of my jeans," Audrey told him.

"Come on, Andy, play fair! I was the one who climbed down into the hole to get it. And I won't lose it." Nathan held out his hand.

Audrey gave him the watch. Nathan looked at it hard and put it to his ear. The ticking didn't seem nearly as loud now. When he was sure that the watch was still going, Nathan pushed it way down into his pants pocket.

Audrey picked up the shopping bag. "Let's go down to the lake to eat lunch. We can feed the crumbs to the ducks."

"And after lunch I'll go fishing." Nathan showed her the little drop-line he carried in a pocket of his jacket.

They pushed their way through thick underbrush to go back down the hill. Audrey looked for the big stump that Nathan had dragged out of the ground. There was a skinny tree growing where she thought the stump had been.

Nathan stayed close to his sister. "Andy, that big hole is gone. The watch sure changed things around here."

No people jogged along the road at the foot of the hill. The road itself was a rutted trail through the woods. Audrey and Nathan crossed it to get to the lake.

They couldn't see the lake, but they were sure it was there. They could hear the loud quacking of a duck.

"There he is, Andy!" Nathan pointed to a duck with a green head. It flew out of a clump of cattails. "I'm going to see if there's a nest there." Nathan started running toward the cattails.

"Leave the nest alone!" Audrey raced after him.

Suddenly someone came from behind, pushed her to the ground, and rushed over to grab Nathan.

Audrey jumped to her feet and ran to help her brother.

3

A boy not much taller than Audrey had grabbed Nathan's shoulders and was pulling him backward. Audrey made a dive for the boy's ankles and pulled him down.

A moment later all three of them were rolling in the weeds on the ground. "You let go of my brother!" Audrey kneeled on the boy's back and tried to rub his nose in the dirt.

The boy was too strong for her. He got to his feet. Audrey dropped off his back.

"Stop!" the boy said. "I was only trying

to keep your brother out of the quicksand!"

"Quicksand!" Nathan said. "What's that?"

"Look!" The boy picked up a stone and threw it toward the cattails. The stone landed on what looked like a patch of moss. It sank out of sight almost at once.

"I've seen grown men and even horses sucked down into it," the boy told them.

"It's a swamp!" Audrey said. "I'm sorry I hit you. I hope I didn't hurt you. Thank you for saving Nathan's life."

"I guess I'd better thank you, too." Nathan looked at the scabbard that hung from the boy's belt. "Is that a real sword?"

The boy pulled out a short sword and waved it in the air. "It's the best part of the uniform," he said, "except for the hat."

Audrey and Nathan saw that the boy was wearing a red and blue coat with a white vest and pants that came just to his knees. Black leggings covered the rest of his legs and fitted over his shoes. They buttoned all the way up the sides. Audrey thought it must take a long time to put them on. "Where's the hat?" she asked.

The boy walked back to the trail through the woods. He picked up a cap with a tall pointed brass front and put it on. "I was carrying it because it's heavy," he said. "I dropped it when I saw your brother going toward the quicksand."

"That looks like a helmet," Nathan said. "You must feel like a knight in armor."

"I used to," the boy told him, "but I don't anymore."

"What's your name? I'm Nathan, and this is Andy."

"I'm called Franz. And I'm happy to meet you." The boy clicked his heels together and made a little bow. "It's hard to find anybody here who speaks German."

"What do you mean, 'German'?" Nathan said. "We're speaking English!"

Franz took off his hat and scratched

his head. Nathan and Audrey noticed that his straight blond hair was tied at the back of his neck with a black ribbon. "It's very strange," he told them. "I can understand you." He thought for a minute. Then he smiled. "I must be learning English. How do I sound to you?"

"You sound as if you've been speaking it all your life," Audrey said. Perhaps Franz was just playing a joke, she thought, or else this was more magic! "Franz," she said, "would you like to have lunch with us?" She walked over to the plastic bag. It lay on the ground where she had dropped it when Franz pushed her down.

"Where's a good place to picnic, Franz?" Nathan asked.

"I know where there's a freshwater spring," Franz said.

"Lead the way," Nathan said. "I'm starved!"

4

THEY sat on a flat rock beside the bubbling spring to eat their picnic. Franz admired the plastic bag. "It looks like oiled silk," he said.

Audrey handed him one of the peanut butter sandwiches her mother had packed. He ate it slowly. "Strange, but very good." He held up the plastic sandwich bag. "I can see right through it!"

"Try one of Mom's BLTs." Nathan gave Franz half a bacon, lettuce, and tomato sandwich.

"I thought Americans never eat tomatoes," Franz said. "They think they're poisonous."

"We eat them all the time." Nathan took a big bite out of his half of the sandwich.

For a while they were too busy chewing to talk. Then Franz jumped off the rock.

He bent over the spring and cupped his hands to drink.

"Stop, Franz! How do you know that water is safe? Drink this instead." Audrey pulled the top off a can of Seven-Up and handed the can down to him.

Franz took a sip. He climbed back onto the rock. "You boys are so good to me. I don't know how to thank you."

Nathan started to laugh.

"What's so funny?" Franz asked.

"It's just that I'm a girl," Audrey said.

Franz stared at her. "You're a girl? But Andy is a boy's name."

"My name is really Audrey," she told him. "But my friends call me Andy."

Franz smiled. "Then I will, too," he said.

Audrey reached into the plastic bag. "We have macaroons for dessert," she said, and passed the box around.

5

WHEN the last macaroon was eaten, and the Seven-Up was all gone, Audrey put the trash into the shopping bag. "I'll drop it into the first wastebasket we come to."

"We'd better start for home," Nathan said.

"What time is it?" Audrey asked him.

Nathan reached into his pocket and took out the old watch. "It's almost three o'clock." He put the watch away again.

"I'd better get back to camp," Franz said. "Which way do you have to go?"

"We live near Church Avenue," Audrey told him.

Franz put on the cap with the brass front. "My camp is not far from there. I'll see you safely out of the woods." He began to march down the trail that wound between the trees. Audrey and Nathan had to walk fast to keep up with him.

The park seemed much bigger than it was that morning. The woods were thick and tangled. They couldn't see into them. A cold wind began to blow. Audrey zipped up her jacket.

"Look, Andy!" Nathan pointed to a dark bird with a red, bald head. The bird sat on a branch that hung over the trail. "What kind of bird is that?"

Audrey looked at the bird's sharp, hooked bill and strong, curved claws. "I don't know, but I don't like the looks of it."

Franz stopped marching to look up at the bird. "That's a buzzard. It won't hurt you. There were a lot of them circling over these woods after the battle. Now that most of the dead and wounded have been found and taken away, you don't see so many of those birds." Franz began to march even faster than before.

"What battle?" Nathan whispered in his sister's ear.

Audrey didn't answer. She looked at the woods around her and began to walk faster.

After a while the woods were not so thick. The trees had been cut here and there, and the underbrush was cleared away.

Farther along, they came to a field. Nathan and Audrey saw the remains of burned haystacks. On the other side of a row of trees, there was another field. A woman and a girl about Audrey's age were digging for something, although the field had already been picked over. Both the woman and the girl wore long dresses and sunbonnets. The woman pulled out a small potato and dropped it into a sack. She looked up as Franz marched past.

Audrey was right behind him. She waved.

"Hi!" Nathan called.

The woman acted as if she neither saw nor heard them, but the girl stuck out her tongue.

Audrey felt as if she'd been slapped in the face.

The trail was a narrow dirt road now. It wound between fields and patches of woods. They came to a farmhouse. A man with a red badge on his hat was mending a fence. He stood up and bowed to Franz as he went by.

When they reached a crossroads, Franz stopped marching. "Here's Church Lane. Now you should be all right."

"This doesn't look anything like Church Avenue," Nathan said.

"This is the only Church Lane I know," Franz told him.

Nathan looked at the narrow lane. Then he turned to look back at the dirt road they had been following. "Andy, what'll we do?"

"Give me the watch, Nathan." Audrey held out her hand.

Nathan took out the watch and handed it to her.

6

THE watch was still ticking.

Audrey pried open the glass that covered the dial. She touched the big hand and tried to move it ahead. "I can't budge it."

"Give it to me." Nathan took back the watch. He shook it and blew on the hands. Then he tried to push the big hand. It didn't move.

Franz glanced at the watch. "Don't break it!" He looked at the sun. "I'm sure that's the right time. What are you trying to do?"

"We want to go home," Audrey told him. "The watch took us out of our own time and brought us here. Now it won't take us back where we belong."

For what seemed an age, Franz just looked at them. Then he said, "Is this true?"

Both Nathan and Audrey nodded.

"It's not wise to meddle with witch-craft," Franz said in a low voice.

"We didn't do it on purpose," Nathan said.

"And we didn't know what had happened at first. When you talked about a battle, I remembered that there are soldiers buried in a graveyard in the park," Audrey told Franz. "Those soldiers died more than two hundred years before Nathan and I woke up this morning."

Franz thought about this. Suddenly he laughed. "Two hundred years!" he said. "Did it take Americans that long to learn to eat tomatoes? Now I understand why everything in that lunch was new to me!"

"It's not funny, Franz. We don't have anywhere to stay." Nathan put the watch back into his pocket.

They heard the sound of voices and the tread of marching feet. Three tall men came around a bend in the lane. One was

wheeling a barrow loaded with baskets of
corn and bags of flour. Another man carried a squawking chicken under each arm.
All three were wearing blue and red uniforms and tall brass hats.

"Hey there, drummer boy!" a man drag-
ging a fat hog by a rope called to Franz.

Franz clicked his heels and saluted.

"There's a cow at that farm over there."
The man pointed down the lane. "You can
save me the trip back. Go get it and bring
it to camp before suppertime. Quick now,
march!"

Franz saluted again and marched swiftly
toward the farmhouse. Nathan and Audrey
raced after him.

The three soldiers went the other way.

When he reached the farmhouse, Franz opened the wooden gate and walked into the yard. A young woman came out of the house. She had a little white cap on her head, and her long dress came almost to her ankles. The woman was carrying a baby. Two little boys came out after her.

Franz clicked his heels and bowed. "I've come for the cow," he said.

"Your comrades have taken everything they could carry," the woman told him. "I don't know how I will feed my children. Please don't take my cow, too."

"I'm sorry for you," Franz said, "but I must obey my orders." He marched over to the barn and went inside. A few minutes later he came out, leading a spotted cow.

Audrey and Nathan had followed Franz into the farmyard. Now Audrey walked over and laid her hand on his arm. "Franz," she said, "you know you can't do this."

Franz bit his lip. He didn't look at

Audrey. She kept her hand on his arm.

For a few minutes Franz just stood there. Then he turned around and took the cow back into the barn. He came out and shut the barn door behind him.

Once more Franz clicked his heels and bowed to the farm woman. She started forward and held out her arms to hug him. But Franz marched quickly back to the gate and out into Church Lane.

Nathan and Audrey hurried after him.

7

NOBODY said anything for a while. Franz was walking much faster than before. It was all Nathan and Audrey could do to keep up with him. At last Nathan said, "Slow down a bit, Franz."

Franz walked slower. "I don't think you understand what I've done."

"You just did what was right," Audrey said.

"I disobeyed orders. I can be whipped for that." Franz stopped walking and turned to face Audrey and Nathan. "And now I'm a deserter. If I'm caught, they'll hang me."

Audrey felt a cold chill run down her back. She couldn't say a word.

"They can hang you? Then why did you ever join the army in the first place?"

Nathan asked. "Didn't your mother and father try to stop you?"

"They both died of smallpox two months before I enlisted," Franz said. "When I was offered the post of drummer, it seemed a stroke of good fortune. And you should see that drum!" His eyes shone. "It's polished brass, with blue and white rims, and a white leather strap." Franz stopped talking.

"Weren't you afraid of being killed?" Audrey asked.

"I thought it would be a glorious way to die, with bands playing and flags flying," Franz told them. "Besides, my country wasn't fighting anybody. The soldiers just marched in parades.

"But army life is boring, with nothing to do. When we set sail for America, I thought it would be exciting. Instead everybody was seasick."

Suddenly he took off his heavy cap and

threw it into the dusty road. "There's nothing glorious about this war. We're killing a lot of farmers. They don't have uniforms. Most of the time they don't even have guns. And they're not really our enemies. Our king just rented us to the English because they don't want to fight their own war."

"Where's your camp?" Audrey picked up the brass-fronted cap and hid it in the shopping bag. "We'd better get as far away from it as we can."

"Camp is on the outskirts of Flatbush village," Franz told her. "We're headed the other way."

They passed two men loading hay into a wagon. Both of them had red badges in their hats. The children waved to the men and they waved back.

"The people with those red things in their hats are friendlier than the others," Nathan said.

"They're loyal to the English king." Franz started walking faster. "I hope they won't remember that they saw me."

When they came to a little patch of woods between two fields, Audrey said, "This looks like a good place."

"For what?" Nathan asked.

"I'll show you." Audrey stepped into the wood. Nathan and Franz followed her to a hollow, where the vines and underbrush hid them from the road.

Audrey put down the shopping bag. She took the Swiss army knife her father had given her out of the pocket of her jeans. There was a little scissors on the knife. "Give me your coat, Franz."

Franz took off the blue coat and handed it to her. He watched Audrey snip off the brass buttons and the red facing. "It was such a beautiful coat," he said.

"I know, Franz." Audrey gave it back to him and put the buttons and the red cloth into the shopping bag. "But now you don't look so much like a runaway drummer boy."

Nathan looked at Franz. "You'd better take that fancy stuff off his collar and cuffs, too, Andy. And while you're at it, give him a haircut."

8

NATHAN rubbed damp leaves from the ground on Franz's white breeches. "Now you don't look as if you're ready for a parade."

Audrey wanted Franz to leave the short sword in the woods, but he couldn't bear to part with it. He promised to keep it hidden under his coat.

When the three children came out of the little woods onto the dirt road, the sun was getting low in the sky.

"I'm getting hungry," Nathan said.

"So am I," Franz told him. "It's too bad we finished all your mother's BLTs."

"Maybe there's a store where we can buy something to eat." Audrey felt in her pocket. She took out two subway tokens. "This is all I have."

Franz looked at the tokens. "They're not coin of the realm. But don't worry. The regiment was given a month's back pay on Friday. I've got plenty of money."

The road wound through flat woods and fields. Now and then the children passed a farmhouse built of wood shingles. The sun went down. And still they hadn't come to a village. The sky was still pink, but soon it would be dark.

"Look!" Nathan pointed. "There's a farm. Maybe they'll let us sleep in the barn."

"That's a good idea," Franz told him. He took a leather purse out of his coat pocket. "Take this, Andy. You can do the talking. I'm still not sure whether I'm speaking English or you can understand German. I'm afraid if I say anything they'll know I'm a Hessian. If they're loyal to the king, they'll report me for a runaway. If they're not, they'll hate me because I came over to fight them."

Audrey took a silver coin out of the purse. There was still enough light for her to see a man's head stamped on the coin.

His hair was tied in back of his neck just as Franz's was before Audrey cut it. "What's this worth?" she asked.

"That's a shilling," Franz told her. "It should buy supper for us all and pay for bed and breakfast, too."

They were coming close to the farm. There was a fence around the house. Audrey put her hand on the gate.

Suddenly there was a loud yelping. Two big dogs raced out of the shadows in the farmyard and leaped toward the gate. Audrey jumped back.

The front door of the house opened. A short, stocky man stood in the doorway. "Just a minute till I get my boots on," he said. He whistled to the dogs. "Down, Hector! Down, Nelly!"

The dogs lay down, one on each side of the walk just inside the gate. They stopped growling, but they kept their eyes on the children.

The man had his boots on now. He

clumped down the walk and opened the gate. "You boys are out late."

Audrey looked up at him. "Please, sir," she said. "Could we buy something to eat? And could we sleep in your barn? We'll pay for that, too."

The man rubbed his chin. "Come into the house, boys. You'd better go around to the side door and leave those dusty shoes on the doorstep there." He opened the gate.

The dogs stood up and wagged their tails. Audrey went into the farmyard and over to the house. Nathan and Franz followed her.

9

THE farmer took off his boots and set them on the doorstep. Audrey and Nathan slipped out of their sneakers and put them beside the boots.

Franz had to unbutton the bottom of his leggings before he could take off his shoes. He put them neatly alongside the sneakers.

The farmer looked at the sneakers and then at the children's clothes. "You're not from around here." He held open the door. "Where are your parents?"

Nathan stepped into the house. "We don't know. We're trying to find them."

Audrey followed her brother, and Franz came right behind her. It seemed strange to be walking in sock feet. They found themselves in a big kitchen, where a plump woman with pink cheeks was standing by a fireplace that went all the way across one wall. Audrey noticed that the woman was wearing slippers.

The farmer put on a pair of slippers, too. "I'm Kurt Bergen," he said. "This is my wife, Catrina."

"My name is Andy Johnson," Audrey said. It was easier to let people think she was a boy than to explain her short hair and blue jeans. "This is my brother, Nathan, and our friend, Franz."

Franz looked as if he were going to click his heels and bow. Nathan stepped on his foot to stop him. The drummer boy held out his hand to the farmer instead.

Kurt Bergen shook Franz's hand. "You boys can put your coats over there." He pointed to a row of pegs on the wall.

Nathan hung up his jacket. Audrey looped the handles of the shopping bag over the next peg and draped her jacket over it. Franz hid the sword and scabbard in the sleeve of his coat before he hung it on a peg.

The farmer's wife was stirring cornmeal mush in a large pot that hung from a hook over the fire. She spooned it into five tin bowls and poured a mixture of skim milk and molasses on top. Then she filled five pewter mugs with cider from the barrel near the door.

It was dark now. Kurt Bergen lit two tallow candles from the cooking fire. He placed them on the long table. His wife set out the bowls of mush and mugs of cider. After that they all sat down to eat supper.

Audrey had never eaten mush before. She didn't like the way it looked, but she was so hungry that it tasted wonderful. Both Nathan and Franz ate every bit in their bowls.

"I hope you had enough to eat, boys," the farmer's wife said. "General Washington's troops drove most of our cattle to Long Island before they left. They burned the hay in the field to keep the British from getting it. Now the Hessians are taking what they want from us. All the smoked meat we'd put away to last the winter is gone. They even carried away the cabbages and potatoes and turnips."

"Oh," Audrey said. "I'm sorry. We didn't know you had so little food." She took two shillings out of Franz's purse and gave them to Kurt Bergen.

"That's too much, Andy," the farmer said. He handed back one of the shillings and put the other into his pocket. "I don't like taking anything from you boys, but right now we need the money."

He picked up one of the candlesticks from the table. "Come with me. I'll show you where you can sleep."

10

Audrey and the two boys went to get their jackets. Then they followed the farmer up a narrow stair to the attic.

There was a big chimney in the center of the room. The floor was made of brick. Audrey looked up and saw iron hooks in the beams overhead.

"This is where we used to hang our hams and smoked beef," Kurt Bergen said. "Those bins are where we kept the grain until we sent it to the mill, and the flour when it came back. The Hessians have carried away most of what we had. They left us the cornmeal. I suppose they don't use it in their country."

The farmer pointed to a pile of empty grain sacks. "These make good pallets." He opened one of the bins. It was full of dry corn husks. "Here's plenty of stuffing."

Kurt Bergen set the candlestick on the brick floor. "Make yourselves at home, boys. Sleep well. I'll see you in the morning." He went back down the narrow stair.

Franz picked up one of the big cloth sacks and began to stuff it with corn husks. "At home we use straw," he said.

Audrey and Nathan watched him for a minute. "You'd better get busy before the candle goes out," Franz told them. "Or do you want to sleep on these hard bricks?"

"Oh! Now I understand! You're making a mattress!" Audrey took a sack off the pile and handed one to Nathan. They both started to fill the sacks with corn husks.

"I want to make a pillow," Nathan said, when he had crammed his sack with stuffing.

"That's a good idea." Audrey finished packing corn husks into her sack. She partly filled another sack, rolled it into a fat lump, and covered it with her jacket. This was her pillow.

"I thought we'd need our jackets for

bed covers," Nathan said, "but the chimney keeps this room warm."

"Too warm." Audrey went to open one of the two small windows in the attic. She looked out at the night sky. A full moon was rising above the trees. She could hear the hoot of an owl over by the barn.

Franz had made a neat pallet for himself. He put the sword near it on the floor.

Nathan laid his bed alongside, and Audrey's was next to his. The children decided to sleep in their clothes. When they were all in bed, Franz blew out the candle. "We shouldn't waste it," he said.

Nathan fell asleep almost at once, but Audrey lay awake and watched the shadows the moonlight made in the attic. She wondered if their mother and father were looking for her and Nathan. It was almost as if they were like Franz, who didn't have a mother and father. But Audrey and Nathan had each other; Franz was all alone in the world.

She wondered if the drummer boy was awake, too. "Franz," she whispered.

"Yes," he answered.

"I'm sorry I got you into all this trouble," Audrey said. "I didn't know what I was doing when I told you not to obey that soldier."

"Andy," Franz said in a low voice. "It was the best thing I ever did. Now be quiet and go to sleep."

11

SOMEONE was shaking Audrey. She opened her eyes, expecting to see her mother. Instead she looked up into the round, pink face of Catrina Bergen. The morning sunlight was streaming through the little attic windows. Audrey could hear the dogs barking out in the yard.

"Get up, Andy!" the farmer's wife whispered. She was holding a pile of clothes. "There are three soldiers at the gate. They're looking for a runaway drummer. Make that Hessian boy put these on." She handed Audrey a long blue dress and a white cap. "They said he's with two strange boys. You and your brother had better change your clothes, too." Catrina Bergen laid two more dresses and two caps across the foot of Audrey's bed. She went to the top of the stair and stood there. "Hurry!"

Nathan and Franz were both awake and sitting up in bed now.

Audrey put her finger to her lips. "Did you hear?"

Nathan nodded, but Franz shook his head. Audrey gave her brother a bright red dress and one of the caps. She picked up the blue dress and went over to Franz. "They're looking for you," she whispered. She slipped the blue dress over his head. It was too big and easily went over his shirt and breeches. Audrey hooked it up the back. "Roll up those buttony things on your legs." She pulled the white cap over his ears and tucked his yellow hair out of sight.

Nathan was already in the red dress. It came down so far that it covered the bottom of his jean legs.

The farmer's wife tiptoed back from the top of the stair. She picked up the checked red and black dress that was still on Audrey's bed. Audrey held her arms in the air, and Catrina pulled the dress down over her clothes. She buttoned up the dress and set the little cap on Audrey's head.

The farmer's wife smiled. "Anyone would think you're a girl. Just be careful how you walk."

"No marching, Franz!" Nathan whispered.

Catrina Bergen picked up Audrey's and Nathan's jackets and the shopping bag. She hid the children's things under the corn husks in the bin.

Audrey pulled the sword in its scabbard

away from Franz. She wrapped it in his coat and shoved them both far down under the corn husks.

The dogs had stopped barking. Audrey held her breath. She heard the kitchen door open and close. There was the sound of men's voices and the clomp of heavy boots downstairs.

"What's up this stair?" she heard a man ask.

"My children are asleep there," Kurt Bergen told him.

"Show me!" the man said.

"Catrina," Kurt Bergen called in a loud voice. "See that the children are decent. I'm bringing a man upstairs."

In a few moments the farmer stepped into the attic. He was followed by a soldier in a blue and red uniform and a tall brass hat. Audrey was sure it was the same one who had ordered Franz to go after the cow yesterday.

"These are my daughters," Kurt Bergen said.

Audrey made the little curtsy she had learned in dancing school. Nathan bent his knees and ducked his head. But Franz stood quite still as if he were made of ice.

The soldier walked over to Franz. "You're strong looking for a girl," he said.

Franz didn't answer.

Audrey knew she had to do something. But what could she do?

12

THERE was no time to lose. Audrey pushed her way between Franz and the tall Hessian. She turned to face the soldier.

"Of course she's strong—strong and nasty, and ugly! And do you know why?" Audrey was so frightened that her voice was a hoarse whisper. "It's because she takes second and *third* helpings at dinner. She's a pig, and I hate her!"

Catrina Bergen threw her arms around Franz. She held him close so that his big hands were hidden in her apron. "Don't mind your little sister, my darling," she cooed. "She's just jealous of your beautiful hair." The farmer's wife stroked a strand of Franz's yellow hair that stuck out from under the cap.

The Hessian was staring down at Audrey. She didn't know what she was going to say, but she *had* to go on talking.

"Take her away with you, soldier," Audrey begged. "She's a thief! She stole the red shoes from my Barbie doll."

Nathan remembered this was something he had done long ago when they were both much younger.

"And, what was worse, she *cut Barbie's hair!*" Audrey said.

Nathan had done this, too. Audrey had been very upset when Nathan cut her doll's hair. He had thought it would grow back.

It was awful to hear Audrey accuse Franz. Nathan didn't think he could stand it much longer. He went over to Kurt Bergen. Nathan was trying to walk like a girl, and his sock feet kept getting tangled in the hem of the red dress. "Daddy," he whined, "let's go downstairs."

"Catrina," the farmer said to his wife, "aren't you ashamed of your daughters?"

He turned to the soldier. "My wife spoils the children. If they were boys, I'd whip them, but I can't hit girls." He patted Nathan's white cap. "This little one is the best of the lot, but I'm afraid my wife will spoil her, too."

"You have a kind face, soldier," Audrey said. "Take me away from these terrible people. They're not my real parents. They stole me when I was a baby. My father is very rich. He will give you a lot of money when you take me back to him."

Audrey liked this story. She began to talk in a louder voice. But the Hessian raised his head to look at Franz.

"Yes," Audrey cried out, "look at her in that beautiful dress! It's *my* dress, soldier! Make her take it off this minute!" She grabbed both his hands. "Oh, please, please, make that girl give me back my dress!"

The soldier was standing as tall and

stiff as he could. "In my country this would never be allowed."

At that moment two more soldiers came up the stairs into the attic. "What are you doing to the little girl, Hermann?" one of them said. "I never heard such cries."

The other soldier started to look in all the bins. "There's no sign of those boys anywhere in the house. We're just wasting time here."

Audrey let go of Hermann's hands. He was so glad to get away from her that he forgot to look closer at Franz. He walked back to the stairs. "Better search the barn," he said. "They've got to be somewhere between here and New Utrecht."

The soldier turned to Kurt Bergen. "I'm sorry for you," he said. "I hope I have only sons when I marry."

13

AUDREY watched from the attic window as Kurt Bergen and his wife waved good-bye to the soldiers. She waited until the three tall men were out of sight before she took off the checked dress and the little cap. Then she unhooked the blue dress Franz was wearing and pulled it over his head. Nathan had no trouble getting out of the baggy red dress. It was much too big for him.

Audrey folded the dresses and the little caps and put them in a neat pile. She carried the clothes down to the kitchen.

Catrina Bergen was cooking something in an iron skillet set over the glowing coals in the big fireplace. She took a cornmeal pancake out of the skillet and added it to the stack keeping warm in the brick Dutch oven. "Put those clothes on the dresser, Andy."

Audrey did as she was told. "How can I thank you?" she asked.

"Don't thank me. Just take my advice," the farmer's wife said. She opened a chest under one of the windows. "Kurt is too stout for these now, but they'll fit Franz." She handed Audrey a homespun shirt, a worn brown coat, and knee-length breeches. "He should stop wearing that uniform with the turnbacks cut off. And he'd better get rid of those military gaiters. Here are some stockings I just finished. I'll knit another pair for Kurt."

Audrey started toward the attic stairway. "Be sure Franz puts those on," Catrina said. "And give his beautiful clothes to me."

Franz changed out of his uniform without an argument, but he insisted on keeping the tall cap with the brass front and the sword and scabbard. Audrey got out the shopping bag to pack them in.

She reached in and took out the red turnbacks, the brass buttons, and the blue and white ribbons she had cut off Franz's coat. "I promised Mrs. Bergen I'd give her your fancy stuff. While I'm at it, I guess I'd better throw out the trash from our picnic."

"You mean those little shining see-through pouches and the green mugs?" Franz said. "If you don't want them, I do. I've never seen anything like them. You can't tell when they might come in handy."

It seemed silly to save sandwich bags and Seven-Up cans, but Audrey didn't want to hurt Franz's feelings by laughing at him. She took out the scrunched paper napkins and the empty macaroon box. "At least I can throw these things away."

Franz looked at them. "You'd better keep that, too, Andy. Sometimes a bit of paper is hard to get."

Audrey looked around the attic. Franz was right. She couldn't see a scrap of paper anywhere there. She smoothed the napkins and put them back into the plastic shopping bag with the macaroon box.

Nathan was looking out of the little window. "There's a row of hills over there. Maybe we should head that way."

Audrey and Franz craned their necks to look out of the window, too.

"Andy, look!" Nathan pointed to a grove of trees. A man was just stepping out of it. He walked slowly across a burned field and came into the farmyard.

It was Kurt Bergen. He was carrying a pail of milk in each hand.

14

CLANG! Clang! Clang! Catrina Bergen was banging the bottom of a copper pot with an iron spoon. "Breakfast time!" she called.

Audrey, Nathan, and Franz almost fell over each other running down the narrow attic stairway in their stocking feet.

The long table was set with blue and white plates. There was a bowl of purple asters in the middle. Catrina served the cornmeal pancakes with butter and blackberry jam.

"This feast is in your honor, Franz," Kurt Bergen said. "The Hessians told me how you ran away after they sent you to take Gitty Jane's cow."

"Did they take the cow away from her after all?" Audrey wanted to know.

"They couldn't find it," the farmer said between bites of pancake. "They think Franz took it and sold it. Gitty Jane must have found a place to hide it."

"I thought General Washington's army drove all the cattle to Long Island," Nathan said.

"They let *us* keep one cow. We promised to hide her so the British and Hessians couldn't get her," Catrina Bergen said. "We tied Phoebe where there are lots of weeds to eat." She laughed. "I wish she didn't like wild onions so much."

"Is that why the butter tastes funny?" Nathan asked.

The farmer's wife nodded. She turned to Franz. "You'll be much safer if nobody finds that uniform."

"What are you going to do with it?" Franz said.

"It will look beautiful in the patchwork quilt I'm making," Catrina told him.

"What about the buttons?" Audrey asked.

"They'll go into my button box," Catrina said. "One of these days I'll find a use for them."

"Don't you ever throw anything away?" Nathan asked.

"Not if it can be used for anything," Kurt Bergen told him. "Waste not, want not."

Nathan started to say, "That's what Mom says." He stopped in the middle of the sentence.

When breakfast was over, the children took their shoes off the doorstep and put them on. They walked over to the well near the kitchen door. Beside it was a wooden bucket tied to a rope. Franz let the bucket down into the well and pulled it up full of water.

Nathan helped lift the bucket over the rim of the well. "Andy, do you still have those empty Seven-Up cans?"

Audrey took the four cans out of the plastic bag. Nathan rinsed them and filled them with fresh water. He stuffed the holes in the tops with bunches of mint leaves that grew near the well.

Audrey propped the cans upright between the sword and the brass hat. She had taken out the cookie box and was just going to put it back into the plastic bag when Catrina Bergen opened the kitchen door.

"Andy, bring that box here," the farmer's wife called.

Audrey saw that she was holding a pan of cornbread.

"I was wondering how you were going to carry this," Catrina Bergen said. "That looks like just the thing." She packed the cornbread in the empty macaroon box. Then she gave a big red apple to each of the children. They stuffed them into their pockets.

Catrina went into the kitchen and came out with a wedge of yellow cheese wrapped in a lettuce leaf. She tucked it into the shopping bag.

It was time to say good-bye. Kurt Bergen shook their hands, and his wife hugged them.

"You'd better stay off the roads," the farmer said. "Cut through the fields. And good luck!"

15

AT first the fields were flat, then there were hills and more trees. At lunchtime the three children sat under a big sycamore tree to eat some of the food Catrina Bergen had given them.

After lunch Nathan climbed the tree.

"Let's walk to the west," he told Audrey and Franz. "There's water over there."

They went through a woods and came out onto a road along a cliff. "That's Staten Island!" Franz pointed to it. "Those ships in the bay down there are British. There must be Hessians around here. Somebody will be sure to know me. I'd better get away."

Audrey and Nathan followed him down from the cliff. They walked along the marshy shore between rough little hills of sand. Audrey almost lost her sneakers in the soft, wet ground. She took them off and went barefoot. Before long both Nathan and Franz had their shoes off, too. They all took turns carrying the shopping bag.

The children waded across a creek and made their way through patches of grass higher than their heads. When they came to a beach, Nathan said, "This looks like a great place to go fishing!"

Audrey pointed down the sand to where there were men with fishing nets. "Someone else thinks so, too. Come on, Nathan. You'll have to find another place to fish."

After a while they came to an arm of the bay with an island on the other side. "There are woods over there," Audrey said. "If we swam to it, we'd have a good place to hide."

Franz didn't know how to swim, but Nathan saw a boat upside down in the reeds. The children turned it over and pushed it into the water.

"Get in," Audrey told the boys. "I'll be the outboard motor."

She took off everything but her underwear and swam behind the boat until they reached the shore where the pine trees grew. "If we don't put the boat back where it was, someone will start looking for it."

Nathan wanted to have the fun of swimming the boat back. Audrey went with him. They put it back in the reeds where they had found it. Without Franz to help them, it was much harder to turn over.

Audrey was tired when at last they had the boat in place. She swam on her back all the way to the piny shore. Nathan splashed after her.

"I wish I could swim like that," Franz said.

It was warm for September. Audrey and Nathan didn't want to put dry clothes over their wet underwear. They put on their socks and sneakers and carried their clothes.

Franz was wearing his shoes and stockings now, too. He took charge of the shopping bag.

They walked through groves of short, twisted trees. Pine needles were thick underfoot, but the ground was sandy.

"What's that noise?" Franz asked.

Nathan and Audrey stopped walking to listen. They heard the steady boom, boom, boom of the ocean beating against the shore.

16

AUDREY, Nathan, and Franz stepped out of the pine woods onto a wide white beach. In front of them the gray Atlantic stretched as far as they could see.

"There's nobody else here. I'm going fishing!" Nathan pulled the little drop-line out of his jacket pocket. He kicked off his sneakers and hung his shirt on a bush.

Franz used his short sword to cut a branch from a young tree for a fishing rod. Nathan tied his line to it. He raced across the wet sand and pulled out a slippery sand eel. "Just what I need for bait!"

Audrey didn't want to see her brother bait his hook. "Come on, Franz. I'll teach you to swim." She ran to the edge of the water and jumped into the surf.

Franz took off the bulky clothes Catrina Bergen had given him. He was wearing

white cotton underpants that came almost to his knees and were tied with a drawstring around his waist.

Franz watched Audrey jumping over and diving under the whitecaps. He waded into the white foam. A wave knocked his feet out from under him. Another splashed him in the face.

Audrey coasted over to him on her stomach. "Isn't this fun?"

Franz grinned. A huge wave curled over his head. He ducked under the wave and let it roar on toward the beach.

The sea was not so rough out beyond the breakers. Audrey showed Franz how to tread water and float on his stomach. "The rest is easy," she said.

Nathan was fishing from a sandbar. He swung his rod and sent the line flying across the deep water on the ocean side of the bar. Splash! Down went the sinker. Nathan felt something pull on his bait. He leaned back and jerked the rod into the air. "I've got a fish!" he screamed. "And it's big enough to feed all of us!"

The three children changed out of their wet underwear into their dry outer clothes. Then they scraped a hole in the sand and filled it with stones. There was plenty of driftwood on the beach. They stacked it beside the fireplace they had made.

Nathan made a little tent of twigs. He felt in his pockets. "Andy, I don't have any matches! We can't light the fire."

Franz laughed. "Why don't you carry a tinder box?" He pulled an iron box out of his coat pocket and took out a steel bar. Franz rubbed the bar against a piece of flint that was fixed to the inside of the box. A spark flew onto some bits of charred cloth in the box. It glowed a moment and went out.

Audrey pulled one of the used paper napkins from the shopping bag. She twisted it into a tight little stick. "Try this, Franz."

In a few minutes the campfire was burning. Audrey hung the wet underwear near it to dry. Nathan borrowed her knife to clean his fish.

"When you're finished with Andy's knife, Nathan, lend it to me."

After he had cleaned the fish, Nathan scoured the knife with sand and wiped it on the rough grass of the dunes. "Here you are, Franz."

Franz pulled his cap out of the shopping bag. He used the scissors on the knife to cut the cap away from its tall brass front.

"What are you doing to your beautiful hat, Franz?" Audrey asked.

Franz laid the brass front of the cap over the coals of the fire. "We need something to cook the fish in," he said.

17

AFTER supper, Franz said, "We'd better build a shelter before it gets dark."

"Andy," Nathan said, "remember the underground house we built last year in the country? Maybe we can show Franz how we made that."

"We'll need something to dig with," Audrey reminded him. "I saw some big clam shells on the beach." She ran to get them.

They all began to scoop a hollow in the ground between the sand dunes and the pine woods. When the hole was big enough for all three to lie down in, Franz shored up the sides with driftwood. "We don't want these sandy walls to cave in," he said.

Audrey made a soft carpet of young, green pine needles. Franz used his sword

to cut reeds and branches. Then they all laid pine branches across the top of the hole to make a roof. They stuffed the spaces between the branches with reeds. At one end of the roof they left an open space for a door.

The cooking fire was still glowing. Franz threw sand on it to put it out. It was cold by the ocean. Their underwear was dry now and the children put it back on.

The light was almost gone from the sky. They packed everything into the shopping bag and took it into the shelter. From outside, the little hut looked like a pile of branches and broken reeds.

Nathan was in the middle with Audrey on one side and Franz on the other. They were all so tired that they fell asleep as soon as they lay down.

Audrey was awakened by the morning sun shining through the open space in the roof. For a moment she didn't know where she was. Then she heard the surf pounding on the beach and the screams of the seagulls overhead.

The boys were both fast asleep. Audrey wiggled over to the door in the roof and climbed out into the open air.

She took off her sneakers and socks, rolled her jeans above her knees, and ran across the wide, wet beach to the water. The cool waves lapped at her bare feet.

Audrey walked into the surf. She felt a hard lump under her foot. It must be a stone, she thought. They could use it in the cooking fire. Audrey leaned over and dug out the lump.

It was a clam.

"That's one way to find clams," she heard a deep voice say.

Audrey was so startled that she nearly dropped the clam. She looked around. There was no one on the beach.

Then she caught sight of someone half-hidden by a tall clump of reeds. Whoever it was seemed to be kneeling on the ground and digging for something.

Audrey felt that she had better find out who it was before Franz got up. And she had to warn him that there was someone else on the island.

"Good morning!" she yelled across the beach.

"A good morning to you!" came the deep-voiced answer.

Audrey hoped that the boys had heard, but she couldn't be sure. She held onto the clam and walked over to the reeds.

18

WHEN Audrey came close to the clump of reeds, she saw a woman in a gray bonnet. She was wearing a long gray dress that she had tucked up to keep from tripping over it. Beside her on the ground was a flat basket. She was loading it with roots that she was digging from under the reeds.

"These aren't as big as they'll be in the wintertime, but beggars can't be choosers," the woman said. Her brown hair was streaked with gray. It kept falling into her eyes. She pushed it back under her bonnet. Then she looked up at Audrey with bright green eyes.

"What are you going to do with the roots?" Audrey asked.

"I'll either roast or boil them," the woman told her.

"Why?" Audrey asked.

The woman stood up and pulled her dress down to her ankles. Audrey saw that she was tall and lean. "They taste better that way. I never heard that they were very good raw."

"I didn't know you could eat them at all," Audrey said.

"Neither did I till an Indian told me. Indians eat a lot of things other people don't." The woman reached up and grabbed the tassels on the reeds with her strong hands. She shook the little red seeds on the tassels into her apron. "Indians make porridge out of these." She filled her apron with seeds. "What's your name, lad? I'm Elizabeth Lake."

"My name is Andy Johnson," Audrey told her.

"Well, Andy," Elizabeth Lake said, "would you please untie my apron?" She turned around so Audrey could do it. Then she wrapped the apron around the seeds and put it in her basket. "Are you going to eat that clam, Andy?"

"I would if I knew how to cook it," Audrey said.

"That's easy." Elizabeth Lake left her basket on the ground and walked over to the beach. "But one clam isn't much good. Let's see if we can find some more." She began to stamp along the wet sand.

Audrey saw a little jet of water spurt up into the air.

"Dig there!" Elizabeth Lake told her.

Audrey dug with one hand where the water had spurted. She pulled out a clam. Now she had a clam in each hand. "I'll go get something to put these in." She ran over to the shelter behind the dunes.

Nathan and Franz were still asleep. Audrey unpacked the shopping bag and left everything in the hut. Then she put the two clams into the empty bag and took it to the beach.

Elizabeth Lake had taken off her shoes and stockings, and tucked up her skirt again. She was wading in the surf. "I thought I'd try your way. It looked like such fun," she said. "Ouch!" She leaned way over and pulled a crab out of the water.

"Did he hurt you?" Audrey went over and held open the plastic bag.

"Don't worry. We'll get even with him." Elizabeth Lake dropped the crab into the bag.

Audrey decided to stamp on the beach and dig up the squirting clams there. Elizabeth Lake stepped on the crabs and clams in the shallow water. Together they filled the plastic bag all the way to the top.

"I'll show you how to steam them," Elizabeth Lake said. "First we'll dig a pit and make a fire. Then we'll have to heat some stones and put seaweed on them along with the clams and the crabs."

Audrey ran to the pile of pine branches behind the dunes. "Get up, lazybones! If you want steamed clams for breakfast, you have to build a fire."

19

"MISTRESS LAKE," Franz said, "we're almost out of drinking water. Do you know where we can find some?"

"I'm not sure if the water here on the island is safe," she said. "If you boys come with me, you can have all the water you want from my well. But please call me Elizabeth. Friends don't use titles."

They feasted on crabs and clams. Afterward, when Nathan and Franz heard how easy it was to catch them, they went out and filled up the shopping bag again. They gave the shellfish to Elizabeth.

"Thank you," she said. "You can carry your present home for me when you come to get your drinking water."

"Where do you live?" Audrey asked.

"In Gravesend," Elizabeth Lake told her.

"Are there Hessian soldiers there?" Franz wanted to know.

"There are Hessians everywhere." Elizabeth Lake looked at his face. "Why do you ask, Franz?"

Franz turned away from her. "I'm a Hessian myself, a deserter from the army."

Elizabeth Lake touched his arm. "You don't seem at all like a Hessian," she said. "Your speech is just like that of your friends. It's not the way we talk around here, but it certainly doesn't sound German. Anyway, I am *glad* you deserted! Friends don't believe in war." She picked up her basket. "Come along." Elizabeth Lake started walking toward the pine woods.

"Wait a minute!" Audrey went to get the Seven-Up cans.

Nathan and Franz each took a handle of the shopping bag. Between them they carried the heavy load of shellfish.

When they reached the other side of

the island, Elizabeth Lake showed them her boat pulled up on the bank. It was the same boat the children had borrowed the day before. Elizabeth Lake dragged the oars out from under a fallen tree in the woods nearby.

Audrey, Nathan, and Franz shoved the boat into the water and climbed into it. Elizabeth Lake rowed them across to the mainland.

They left the boat upside-down in the reeds and hid the oars a short distance away. Then Elizabeth Lake took them on a shortcut across the meadows. They circled around the village of Gravesend and came to a small farmhouse built of wooden shingles.

Elizabeth Lake opened the gate in the picket fence. She went up the walk to her front door and unlocked it with a key that hung from her belt. "Come inside, boys."

Audrey, Nathan, and Franz followed

her into the big front room. There was a four-poster bed in one corner and a spinning wheel in another. They saw a round tea table and four ladderback chairs. Audrey noticed a big chest against one wall. The room seemed to be used as a sitting room, bedroom, and workroom.

They walked through it into the kitchen at the back of the house.

Elizabeth Lake put her basket on the kitchen table. "I want to go and see if Fanny and Charlie are all right." She went out of the back door.

"She never told us she had children," Nathan whispered.

"Let's go and meet them," Franz said.

The boys put down the bag of clams and crabs and went outdoors. Audrey came after them. She set the four Seven-Up cans on the stone rim of the well near the door. Then she raced after Nathan and Franz.

ELIZABETH LAKE was walking toward the red barn. Franz, Nathan, and Audrey hurried after her.

Instead of going into the barn, Elizabeth Lake went around the corner of it. The children couldn't see her now, but they could hear her deep voice.

"Fanny," she said, "there's no need to be rude. I told you I'd be home in a little while."

The three children peeked around the corner of the barn. A patch of grass and weeds there had been fenced to make a pen. Inside it a mother goat and her little kid were chewing on a thistle.

Elizabeth Lake looked around. "Fanny's pretending she doesn't know me. I haven't had much time for her lately."

Franz went to the gate of the goat pen and opened it. He walked over to the big goat. "There's a good girl." He gently stroked the goat's head.

Elizabeth Lake stared. "Fanny won't let most people come near her."

Franz went on stroking the goat. "We always had goats on our farm," he said. "Fanny needs to be milked. Where do you keep your pail?"

"Just inside the kitchen door," Elizabeth Lake told him.

Franz ran back to the house and got the pail. He kneeled on the ground to milk the goat. Audrey carried the pail of milk to the kitchen and put it on the table.

When she came out of the house, she saw her brother by the well. "Franz says

Fanny and Charlie need fresh water," Nathan said.

There was a big wooden bucket on the stone rim of the well. It was tied to a rope. When Audrey dropped the bucket into the well, Nathan turned a crank to let the rope unwind.

Splash! The bucket sank into the water. Then Audrey and Nathan took turns cranking the handle to wind up the rope. They pulled the bucket onto the rim of the well.

Audrey filled the Seven-Up cans, and they each took a drink. After that Nathan untied the rope. Together the two children carried the heavy bucket of water to the goat pen. They put it down on a bare patch of ground just inside the gate.

Franz filled a tin pan with water for the goats.

Audrey looked at the bucket. "We'd better take the water back to the house."

"Why carry anything so heavy when there's plenty of water in the well?" Elizabeth Lake poured the water onto the bare ground. "This will help the thistles grow."

Franz took the empty bucket back to the well.

"What's in the barn?" Nathan asked.

"Come along," Elizabeth Lake said.

"You'll see." She led the way around the corner of the red barn and unlocked the big door.

Franz was back from the well. They all went into the barn. There was very little inside it.

"The hay was burned in the fields," Elizabeth Lake told them. "There's corn still on the stalks. I'll have to get busy and pick it before winter comes."

"We can do that for you, Mistress Lake, I mean, Elizabeth." Franz turned red.

Elizabeth Lake looked at him. "Would you rather call me Aunt Elizabeth, Franz?"

"Oh, yes." Franz smiled.

"May Andy and I call you Aunt Elizabeth, too?" Nathan asked.

"It would make me very happy," Elizabeth Lake said.

21

"WE need something to put the corn in, Aunt Elizabeth," Audrey said.

Elizabeth Lake looked around the barn. "I think Joseph kept baskets here. He used to work for me. Joseph went off in a hurry to join General Washington's army. I still haven't put things in order."

She went over to a row of wooden barrels. "We can store the corn in those, but they're too heavy to take out to the field."

Audrey pointed to a stack of round bushel baskets half hidden behind one of the big barrels. "What's that?"

"Just what we're looking for." Elizabeth Lake took down four baskets. She gave one to each of the children and kept one for herself. "Come along." She went out of the barn and started across a bare, burned field.

Audrey, Nathan, and Franz came after her. Franz closed the barn door behind him.

On the other side of the field they came to several rows of trees.

"There are apples on these trees," Franz said. "They should be picked before the first frost."

"Oh," Elizabeth Lake said. "Thank you for telling me. I always left things like that for Joseph."

The cornfield was just behind the apple trees. They all went to work picking the ears of corn.

Nathan peeled back part of the husk of one of them. He felt the hard, dry kernels. "You waited too long to pick these, Aunt Elizabeth. I don't see how you can eat them now."

Elizabeth Lake laughed. "Nathan, that's not corn to eat off the cob. It has to go to the miller to be ground into cornmeal."

When all the baskets were full, they

carried them to the barn and filled a barrel with the ears of corn. Then they went back to pick another load. After three trips to the cornfield and back to the barn, Elizabeth Lake said, "Time for lunch." She led the way to the house.

Before they reached it they all knew that something was wrong. The back door was hanging by one hinge.

Elizabeth Lake stepped into her kitchen. The children came in after her. A chair had been thrown against a wall. The back was broken off. The basket of roots and seeds was still on the table, but the shopping bag was on its side on the floor. There was a pile of clams beside it, and crabs were crawling around the room. All the cupboard doors were swinging open.

They went into the big front room. One of the chairs was overturned. The lid of the big chest was open, and the clothes in it had been tossed onto the floor.

"If they were looking for money," Elizabeth Lake said, "they wouldn't find it in this house." She walked back into her kitchen.

Nathan and Franz began to chase the crabs across the floor. Elizabeth Lake took out a big iron pot. "You can put them in here." She picked up the plastic shopping bag and gave it to Audrey. "You'd better rinse this. It may smell fishy. I'm going to get some water."

Elizabeth Lake went out of the back door. Audrey followed her over to the well. They tied the bucket to the rope and were about to let it down into the well.

Suddenly Elizabeth Lake put her finger to her lips. "Listen!"

Audrey heard a faint bleating sound.

"It's Charlie!" Elizabeth Lake put down the bucket and raced toward the barn.

Audrey ran after her.

22

ELIZABETH LAKE held up her skirt and tore over to the red barn like a whirlwind. It was all Audrey could do to keep up with her.

When they reached the barn, they stopped running and peeked around the corner. They saw three Hessian soldiers with tall brass hats and red and blue coats by the goat pen. Their backs were toward the barn. The two goats were in the center of the pen, facing the soldiers.

Elizabeth Lake turned to Audrey. "Stay out of sight, Andy," she whispered. "Let me handle this myself. Promise!" She looked so hard at Audrey with her bright green eyes that Audrey had to nod.

"That little one would taste good in a

stew," the tallest soldier said. "Go get him, Klaus."

Klaus was short and fat. His round face was pink and covered with freckles. He opened the gate of the pen and stepped inside.

The little goat moved back. Klaus tip-toed toward him. Charlie dodged and leaped for the open gate.

When Klaus turned to follow the little goat, the nannygoat butted him in the seat of his white breeches. Klaus fell facedown into a patch of thistles.

The other two soldiers both rushed to grab Charlie. Clang! Their brass hats crashed together, and their shiny black shoes skidded in the thick mud where Elizabeth Lake had emptied the bucket of water. The tall soldier fell on his hands and knees. The other slid sideways through the mud.

Charlie slipped through the gate and dashed across the burned field toward the apple trees. Fanny was right behind him.

Audrey was going to run after the goats, but Elizabeth Lake started to laugh. She put her hand over her mouth, but she couldn't stop laughing. The soldiers were trying to stand up. They kept sliding on the slippery ground.

"Run, Aunt Elizabeth!" Audrey begged.

Elizabeth Lake looked at her. She stopped laughing at once. "Hide in the barn, Andy!" she commanded. "Quick!"

Audrey slipped into the barn. Elizabeth Lake closed the door from the outside, leaving a crack just wide enough for Audrey to see out.

The three soldiers came around the corner of the barn. Klaus's freckled face was scratched from the thistles, and there were green stains on his breeches. The other two soldiers were smeared with mud.

"What were you laughing about, woman?" the tall soldier asked.

"You looked so funny," Elizabeth Lake told him.

"Say *sir* when you speak to me!" the soldier ordered.

Elizabeth Lake held her head high. "I don't call anybody by a title. Tell me your name, friend, and I'll call you that."

"Don't waste time talking to her," Klaus said. "Can't you see she's one of those crazy Quakers?"

The tall soldier looked at Elizabeth Lake's plain gray dress and bonnet. "I don't care what she is. She can't get away with letting her animals attack the king's soldiers. You'll have to come with us, woman." He grabbed her arm. "March!"

Audrey was watching through the crack in the barn door. She saw Elizabeth Lake walk toward the road. There was a soldier on each side of her and one marching along behind.

23

AUDREY didn't wait until Elizabeth Lake and the soldiers were out of sight. She ran back to the house.

Franz and Nathan were building a fire in the big kitchen fireplace. Audrey burst into the room. She raced to a window that had a view of the road. "Look!"

The boys came over to see why she was so excited. They saw the soldiers in red and blue uniforms around the tall gray figure of Elizabeth Lake marching toward Gravesend.

"Those are Hessians!" Franz said. "Why are they taking Aunt Elizabeth away?"

Audrey told the two boys what had happened. "We'd better catch the goats before they get lost," she finished. "After that we can figure out how to rescue Aunt Elizabeth."

The three children found Fanny and Charlie eating windfall apples under the trees. Franz talked to Fanny while Audrey tied a rope they'd brought from the barn around the nannygoat's neck. Then she led Fanny back to the goat pen. Franz picked up Charlie and carried him back to the pen, too.

Nathan brought along as many apples as he could carry to put into the pen with the goats. "At least *they* got something good out of all this," he said.

Franz untied the rope from Fanny's neck and put it away. When he came out of the barn he was carrying a hammer. "I couldn't find any nails. Do you have my purse, Andy? I'm going to Gravesend village to see what my money can buy."

Audrey pulled the purse out of her jeans and handed it to him. "Do you want us to go with you, Franz?"

Franz thought for a minute. "No, Andy. People will be sure to notice you and

Nathan. Your clothes are so different from what people here wear. Anyway, somebody should stay here to watch the house while Aunt Elizabeth is away."

"Aren't you afraid, Franz?" Nathan asked.

"Of course," Franz told him. "But I want to find out if my English is as good as Aunt Elizabeth says. And most of all I want to learn what has happened to her!"

They followed Franz back to the house. He left the hammer on the broken chair and walked into the big front room.

Franz looked at the clothes that had been dumped out of the chest. "Andy, there's a dress that would fit you. You work wonders when you look like a girl." He opened the front door. "When I come back I want to find you wearing the dress." Franz stepped outside. He turned to look at Audrey. "Please, Andy!" he said.

Franz walked quickly to the gate and off down the road.

Nathan shut the front door. "Franz seems to think you can pull some sort of trick for Aunt Elizabeth like you did to save him. What do you think, Andy?"

Audrey picked up a little gray dress and held it against herself. "Those soldiers would slap me if I tried to talk to them." She took off her jacket and her shirt and jeans. Then she slipped the dress on over her head. "This is just like Aunt Elizabeth's dress, only smaller."

Nathan pointed to the patches on the elbows. "Somebody wore it a lot. It's almost worn out."

Nathan helped Audrey pick up the other clothes from the floor. She folded them neatly and put them back into the chest. Audrey put on a small gray bonnet and wrapped herself in a gray wool shawl.

Nathan held up a pair of shoes with chunky heels and big buckles on them. "Try these."

Audrey put on the shoes. "I can get into them, but they don't feel good." She walked around the room in the heavy shoes. "I'll wear them," she said, "for Aunt Elizabeth's sake."

24

FRANZ was back in less than an hour. "The village is just down the road. It's full of Hessians. They didn't look twice at me, and I could listen to everything they said. Aunt Elizabeth is locked up in a room of the house where the colonel is staying."

"I'm going there," Audrey said.

"I'll go with you," Franz told her.

Audrey didn't want to leave her brother all by himself while she was away. "I'd rather go alone, Franz," she said. "You stay here with Nathan."

Nathan was looking at the saw Franz was holding. "Did you get that in the village?"

Franz nodded. He pulled a handful of nails out of his pocket. "I bought these, too."

"I'll help you put the kitchen door back on its hinge," Nathan said.

"The colonel is staying at the big house on Neck Road," Franz told Audrey. "You can't miss it. They say there's a corporal guarding the front door."

Audrey left the house as fast as she could walk in the clumsy shoes. She didn't want either of the boys to know how frightened she was.

A cool wind blew the dust up from the road. Audrey pulled the shawl around her shoulders and clumped past the burned fields to the little village of Gravesend. When she came to Neck Road she met a man driving a wagon. "Please," Audrey said, "can you tell me where the Hessian colonel is staying?"

The man pointed to a long, low house. "He's quartered over there in the old Van Sicklen place. There's a soldier standing by the door."

Audrey thanked the man. She took a deep breath and walked over to the gate in the picket fence. She was about to open the gate when the Hessian by the front door called out, "Halt! What do you want?"

Audrey was sure she had heard that voice before. She looked hard at the soldier. Suddenly she felt cold all over. It seemed impossible, but this was *Hermann*, the Hessian she had tricked in the Bergen farmhouse. He was a corporal now.

"I want to see Aunt Elizabeth." Audrey spoke slowly, making each word as clear as possible. "My brother and I are hungry. Aunt Elizabeth was taken away before she could cook lunch for us."

Hermann stared at her. Audrey was certain he knew her. She could feel her heart pounding against her ribs.

The door of the house opened. A gray-haired man in the most beautiful uniform Audrey had ever seen stood in the door-way. It was the colonel.

Audrey thought about Aunt Elizabeth.

She stood as tall as she could and held her chin up.

"Corporal," the colonel said, "show the young lady into the house."

Hermann clicked his heels and saluted. The colonel went back inside, and Hermann held the door open for Audrey to go in. She walked past him without a word.

The colonel stood by the fireplace in the parlor. "Sit down, my dear."

Audrey sat in a high-backed wooden chair. The colonel sat in one just like it, facing her.

"Now tell me what has happened," the colonel said. "There have been some very serious charges made against your aunt."

25

THE colonel sat very still and watched Audrey's face as she told her story. She spoke the truth except that she didn't say anything about Franz.

"My brother and I were helping Aunt Elizabeth pick corn," Audrey began. She went on to tell the colonel how they came back to the house to get lunch and found the door off the hinge and the chair broken.

The colonel looked sad.

Audrey told how Aunt Elizabeth heard the little goat bleat and ran to see what was going on. The colonel tried to keep his face very serious when he heard how the goats escaped and all three soldiers had ended up on the ground. But Audrey thought she saw the corner of his mouth twitch.

"Then Aunt Elizabeth started to laugh. She couldn't stop. It made the soldiers angry, so they took her away," Audrey finished.

"I think I understand what happened," the colonel said. "These soldiers were stealing from people they thought would not dare to complain. When their uniforms were soiled, they were afraid they'd be caught and punished. That's why they told me your aunt turned savage animals loose to attack them." He got to his feet and went to the front door.

"Corporal," the colonel said, "go upstairs and bring the prisoner down here. I want to speak to her."

Hermann went upstairs. In a few minutes Elizabeth Lake came down. The corporal walked down the stairs after her. He looked at Audrey and frowned.

"You are free to go, Madam," the colonel said to Elizabeth Lake. "This child has told

me a story that matches yours. I'm sorry
we kept you here so long. If you had let
me know about the children, I would have
sent you home at once.''

Elizabeth Lake didn't answer. She was
staring at Audrey as if she couldn't believe
her eyes.

"I'll take you home, Aunt Elizabeth," Audrey said.

Still Elizabeth Lake was silent.

The colonel turned to Hermann. "This lady seems to be in a state of shock, corporal. I want you to go with her and the little girl and see that they get home safely."

Once again Hermann clicked his heels and saluted.

Audrey looked up into the colonel's face. "Thank you," she said.

He bowed. "I'm glad you came. I did not know what to do about your aunt. I hope all of my men behave properly in the future. Good day to you."

Hermann opened the door. Audrey took Elizabeth Lake's hand and pulled her out into the open air. The sunshine seemed to revive her. She looked hard at Audrey. "That dress looks better on you than it ever did on me," she said.

Audrey turned to Hermann. "She's all right now. You can stay and guard the colonel. We'll be able to go home by ourselves."

"Orders are orders," Hermann said in a harsh voice. "I will follow you until you are safely home."

Elizabeth Lake began to stride along. She grinned when she looked at Audrey in the dress and bonnet. Audrey was afraid she would start to laugh out loud.

Hermann marched behind them. Audrey felt his eyes on her the whole time. She only hoped he wouldn't catch sight of Nathan and Franz.

When they came close to the little farmhouse, the front door opened. The two boys came running down the road to meet them!

26

HERMANN was marching right behind Audrey.

When Elizabeth Lake saw Nathan and Franz, she ran forward to hug them. Audrey couldn't let the Hessian see the boys. She stepped back so suddenly that the Hessian bumped into her. Then she swung around and tripped him. He went sprawling in the dust.

"Oh, I'm so sorry!" Audrey bent down and tipped the soldier's tall brass hat over his eyes. "Are you hurt? Let me brush the dirt off your uniform." She looked up and caught Nathan's eye. Audrey cocked her head toward the house.

Nathan pulled Elizabeth Lake and Franz through the gate and up the walk into the house, while Audrey dusted the Hessian's blue and red coat. He refused to let her brush the dirt off his white breeches.

By this time Hermann was glad to say good-bye and go back to guarding the colonel. Audrey thanked him for taking her and Aunt Elizabeth home. She stood on the road and waved to him until he was out of sight.

Audrey changed back into her own clothes while Elizabeth Lake was making chowder out of the clams and boiling the crabs. They all sat down to eat at the kitchen table.

"You mended the chair so well I'd never know it was broken," Elizabeth Lake told the boys. "I don't know how to thank you, or Andy, who made the Hessian colonel let me go free. I'm sure I can make a place for you three to sleep if you want to stay with me."

Franz's eyes shone. "I could build another room onto the house."

"Aunt Elizabeth needs someone like you to help her with the farm, Franz," Audrey said.

"I can't afford anything right now," Elizabeth Lake said. "But as soon as I make money from the farm, I can pay you."

"Franz," Nathan said. "Stay here with Aunt Elizabeth. Andy and I have to find our mother and father."

Franz shook his head. "When you get back to your parents, I'll come and work for Aunt Elizabeth. But until then I'll go with you."

After lunch Audrey and Nathan rinsed the plastic shopping bag with water from the well. They filled the Seven-Up cans and put them into the bag.

Franz took the saw to the barn.

"We'll come tomorrow to finish picking your corn, Aunt Elizabeth," Nathan told her, "and to get some more drinking water. We want to get back to the beach now."

"There's still time to go fishing," Audrey said.

Franz was back from the barn. "We can bring you some more roots and seeds."

"And maybe you'll show us how to cook them," Audrey said.

Elizabeth Lake smiled. "I'd love to." She walked as far as her front gate with them. Then she gave them each a big hug.

"Good fishing!" She closed her gate and went back into her house.

27

AUDREY, Nathan, and Franz crossed the road to the field on the other side.

"Franz," Nathan said, "what were you doing in Prospect Park when we first met you?"

"Prospect Park? Oh, you mean the Flatbush woods." Franz thought for a minute. "So much has happened since then that I haven't thought about it. At the time it seemed very important."

"Do you remember what it was?" Audrey asked.

"I was looking for the only thing I had that belonged to my father," Franz said. "I dropped it during the battle."

"What was it?" Nathan wanted to know.

"A gold watch," Franz told him. "Many of the officers in our army have watches just like it, but I'd know mine anywhere. It had my father's initials on the back, J.G."

Nathan looked at Audrey and didn't say anything. She knew what he was thinking. *Without the watch they could never go home again!*

Audrey spoke very softly. "Nathan, give Franz the watch. It belongs to him."

Nathan took the old watch out of his pocket. He showed Franz the letters on the back. "Is this it?"

"Yes," Franz said, "but you told me a magic watch brought you here from another time."

"It did," Audrey insisted. "We found it under an old stump in the park. And we were trying to set the time."

Nathan turned the watch over so Audrey could open the glass. She tried to push the big hand forward. "It won't move at all now, but then it started going backward all by itself."

Franz put his ear to the watch. "You've let it run down. It has to be wound every day."

Nathan pulled out the key to his toy monkey.

Franz looked at it. "That's not the watch key."

Nathan tried to fit the key into the hole in the watch face. "It worked before, but now I can't even get it to go in." He handed the watch to Franz. "Anyway, it's your watch."

Franz held the watch in the palm of his hand. He ran his fingers around the gold case and looked again at the letters on the back. "Nathan," he said, "I'd like you and Andy to keep this to remember me by. You've been the best friends I ever had. I know my father would want you to have his watch." He gave it to Nathan. Then Franz took a little gold key out of his leather purse. "Here, Andy. This goes with the watch. You should be able to wind it now."

Nathan held the watch. Audrey opened the face and wound it up. She put the key into her pocket. "It's ticking. What time shall I set it?"

Franz looked at the sun. "It's getting late. It must be after four o'clock."

Audrey started to push the big hand forward. "Hold tight, Nathan! It's spinning again!"

28

THE watch hands were spinning so fast that they made Audrey dizzy. She shut her eyes and held onto Nathan to keep from falling. The dings on the hour and the half hour began to be mixed with a loud rattling and squeaking noise. The sound seemed to come from overhead. It became louder and louder. Then it faded away into the distance.

Audrey opened her eyes. "Where's Franz?"

"I don't see him anywhere," Nathan told her. He was looking at the watch. "It says four o'clock now. And it's stopped turning."

Audrey looked around. "It sure is noisy here."

They were standing on a sidewalk in the shadow of the big steel supports of an elevated train. Cars and trucks rumbled along in front of them.

"We must be back in our own time," Nathan said.

Audrey saw an old house across the street. It was jammed between a warehouse and an office building. The yard was full of trees with ivy climbing over them.

"That's Aunt Elizabeth's house!" she whispered.

"It's bigger than it used to be," Nathan told her.

Audrey nodded. Then she said softly, "Franz must have worked on it. You know he wanted to." She thought for a minute. "We never had time to say good-bye to him."

"At least we have the watch to remember him by." Nathan put it in his pocket. "Andy, we'd better not try to go back. We might get stuck there for good. I want to see Mom and Dad."

"They must be worried about us," Audrey said. "We'd better go home — if we can."

They crossed the street to look at Elizabeth Lake's house. A man in blue jeans was sitting in the side yard reading a newspaper. They couldn't see the red barn anywhere.

Three black and white cats loafed in the sun on the little porch. A short, fat woman came out with a pan of food for the cats. When she caught sight of the children, she walked over to the chain link fence. "Is there something I can do for you?"

"We'd like to know what day of the week this is," Audrey said.

The woman laughed. "You ought to know, unless you've been playing hookey. It's Saturday."

Audrey smiled. "Thank you."

The woman went back into the house.

"Saturday!" Nathan said. "We've only been away four hours! But how are we going to get home, Andy? You know we walked for miles to get here."

They walked to the corner. Audrey looked at the street sign. "McDonald Avenue." She pointed to the train rumbling overhead. "That's the F train!" Audrey took two subway tokens out of her pocket. "These are coin of the realm here."

She slung the shopping bag over her shoulder and started up the iron steps to the train station. "Come on, Nathan. We'll take the train home."

Nathan came up after her. "Maybe Mom will let us keep the refunds on the Seven-Up cans."

OTHER BOOKS BY RUTH CHEW

The Wednesday Witch
The Secret Summer
    (original title:
      Baked Beans for Breakfast)
No Such Thing as a Witch
Magic in the Park
What the Witch Left
The Hidden Cave
The Witch's Buttons
The Secret Tree House
Witch in the House
The Would-be Witch
The Trouble with Magic
Summer Magic
Witch's Broom
The Witch's Garden
Earthstar Magic
The Wishing Tree
Secondhand Magic
Mostly Magic
The Magic Coin
The Witch at the Window